Best Friends Forever?

Angela Shelf Medearis
Illustrated by Robert Papp

AN
APPLE
PAPERBACK

SCHOLASTIC INC.

New York   Toronto   London   Auckland   Sydney
Mexico City   New Delhi   Hong Kong   Buenos Aires

To Evelyn Coleman, Taylor Parker, and
Liz Canales with love and thanks
— Angela Shelf Medearis

ISBN 0-439-52330-3

Text copyright © 2004 by Angela Shelf Medearis.
Illustrations copyright © 2004 by Scholastic Inc.

12 11 10 9 8 7 6 5 4 3 2 1   4 5 6 7 8 9/0
                                                              40

Printed in the U.S.A.
First printing, March 2004

Contents

Chapter One

Big Trouble at Bailey Middle School

I tried to stay awake during history class, but I was really sleepy. It was no use. I decided to close my eyes for just a minute.

"Sharie Johnson! Since you're so sleepy, maybe answering my question will help you stay awake," Ms. Canales said.

My eyes blinked open. What was the question? I think I remember hearing something about parent-teacher conferences and time. The question must have been "What time is the parent-teacher conference?"

"Seven o'clock," I said quickly.

"Your answer is seven o'clock. Are you sure about

1

that?" Ms. Canales said as she walked over to my desk.

I squirmed. By the snickering behind me, I was positive that wasn't the answer. "No, I am not sure," I whispered.

I glanced at my best friend, Hannah. It was a purple day for her. She wore all different shades of purple. Her shoes and socks were deep shades of purple. She had sewn purple beads and ribbons onto her purple blouse. She had huge purple flowers pinned onto her pants. She even had a big purple butterfly perched in her curly red hair. I could see by the look on Hannah's face that I'd messed up.

Ms. Canales cleared her throat. "What do you think, class? Is the answer to my question seven o'clock?"

"Nooooooo," everyone said.

"You're right! My question was for those of you who haven't done very well this semester. I asked who would like to have more time to turn in their history reports. Since you have time to sleep during

2

class, you probably don't need extra time for your history report."

The class giggled.

Lately, I'd been dozing off in school. It's all because of my baby sister, Marcy. She wakes up crying around two a.m. almost every morning. It's driving me crazy!

The bell rang and I scrambled along with everyone else to gather my books. Was I glad this day was over! I bounded toward the door.

"Sharie, wait a minute," Ms. Canales said. "I want to talk to you."

I froze. Kids ran past me. I slowly walked to Ms. Canales's desk.

Hannah stood by the door, waiting for me.

"Hannah, please wait for Sharie outside," Ms. Canales said.

Hannah shrugged and went into the hallway.

I sighed. I was in trouble again. I put my head down.

"I'm sorry, Ms. Canales," I said. "But I'm really tired."

"You should be tired," Ms. Canales said. "Tired of not doing your best in my class. What's wrong? You forget your books, your pens, and your homework. You're either daydreaming or falling asleep in class. Is everything alright at home?"

I hesitated. "What do you mean?"

"The first semester you were doing wonderfully in class. You weren't falling asleep. You always had your homework and your supplies. And your mind didn't wander. Am I right?"

"Yes," I said, wishing I was a magician and could just disappear. "Are you going to tell my parents about this?"

"I have no choice," Ms. Canales said. "I have given you many chances to straighten up. First, I asked you to stop whispering to Hannah."

"I did," I said, lifting my head. "I stopped talking."

"For five minutes. I had to ask you two more times during class."

I dropped my head.

"Then you fell asleep."

"I was . . . I was . . ."

"You were what? Being disrespectful? Not listening? What?" Ms. Canales said. "No more excuses. I will talk with your parents at the conference. Then together we'll figure out a way to get you back on track."

I bit my lower lip. I wanted to say, "I'm not running track," or something else smart-mouthed. But that's part of my problem — I can't seem to control my big mouth. This time, I caught myself and just kept quiet.

"Please don't tell my parents, Ms. Canales," I pleaded. "I'll try to do better, honest!"

Her voice was quiet now, almost a whisper. "You can go, Sharie," she said.

The interrogation was over. I grabbed my backpack and slipped it on. I headed out the door, looking up at the clock on my way out. I had one week, three days, and four hours before the parent-teacher conference. Maybe if I do better by then, Ms. Canales will forget about my behavior. Yeah, right.

Hannah was standing by my locker. "What did she say to you?" she asked.

"Nothing. She just had a question about my homework." Even though Hannah was my best friend, I couldn't tell her what Ms. Canales had said to me. It was too embarrassing.

"What are you doing tonight?" I asked her, knowing that neither she nor I ever really did anything on a school night. But somehow I needed to change the subject.

"Nothing much. What about you?"

"I'll probably spend the night listening to the Screech Doll cry and whine."

"I still can't believe you call your baby sister a Screech Doll."

"All she does is cry," I said.

"You want to come over to my house tonight?" Hannah asked.

"You know I can't."

"We could do our homework together."

"Tonight's my night to babysit. You can come over and help me," I said, hoping Hannah would say yes. She actually likes holding Marcy.

"No, my mom's going to be home early tonight."

I knew that she wouldn't come if her mother were home. She liked spending time with her mother, who often traveled out of town. I used to like being with my mother. But since Marcy came along, I haven't had much time alone with Momma.

I took the bus home. I raced into the house, hoping that Marcy was asleep and I could have a snack and talk to Momma in peace, like I used to.

I threw my backpack on the floor and opened the refrigerator. I grabbed an apple and a carton of milk. Then, holding the apple by its stem with my teeth, I took a glass from the cabinet. I was walking toward the table when — *wham!* — something hit my knees.

"Gimmee," Marcy said as she reached for my apple.

The apple fell out of my mouth and rolled under the table. Marcy crawled after it. I slipped and fell against the refrigerator, dropping the glass and then the carton of milk. The glass shattered and milk spilled all over the floor. Momma ran into the kitchen.

"What on earth! I just scrubbed this floor on my hands and knees," she said, staring at the broken glass and milk. "Where's Marcy? Is she hurt?"

I pointed underneath the table. Marcy was holding my apple.

"Come here, baby," Momma said, scooping Marcy into her arms. "Let Momma make sure that old glass or milk didn't get on my little Marcy-Warcy."

I rolled my eyes. I hate it when Momma talks baby talk.

Momma looked at me. "Don't just stand there, Sharie. This mess needs to be cleaned up. Were you trying to balance stuff again? I've asked you many times not to do that."

"But, Momma," I said, "it was Marcy. She tackled me and that's why I dropped everything."

"Don't blame the baby, Sharie. My goodness, she's only eighteen months old. She doesn't even know what tackling is."

"She did tackle me even if she doesn't know what it means. She ran right up and grabbed me around the knees. Then she pushed me out of her way. That's why I dropped everything."

"She was just happy to see you, that's all," Momma said.

A tear slid down my face. Marcy giggled happily as she played with my apple. It was no use arguing with Momma. Her baby could do no wrong. I got the broom and dustpan and swept up the glass. Then I mopped up the milk.

My problems used to be with my big sister, Sandra. She's the beauty and the brains in the family. She's always making straight A's, winning an honor, or doing something special. My parents were always going on and on about how wonderful she is. Then last year, I started to do better in school and at home. But along came Marcy the Screech Doll. Now my parents are always swooning over her.

I put away the mop and broom and went upstairs to do my homework. What a day!

Chapter Two

The Screech Doll

During dinner, I didn't mention my horrible day at school. I ate in silence. Nobody cared — they were too busy listening to Sandra talk about winning the election for eighth-grade Class President.

"Who cares?" I said under my breath. That got their attention, and a lecture from Daddy about my attitude.

I was glad when Daddy told me to go do my homework. I needed to get away from all of them. It didn't last long. I'd just finished my math problems and pulled out my history book when someone pulled on my shirt.

"Stop," I said. "Leave me alone. I'm doing my homework."

"Swingy!" Marcy said, pulling on my arms with her chubby little hands.

"Momma," I yelled. "I'm trying to do my homework and Marcy is bothering me."

"Swingy, swingy, pwese!" she said as she climbed on me.

"Get off of me!" I screamed, just as Momma walked in the room.

"Don't scream at the baby. Just ask her to get down. Why are you being so difficult?" Momma said.

"I'm not. I'm trying to do my homework like Daddy said. And she's in the way."

"Come on, Marcy," Momma said, holding her arms out. "Sharie doesn't want to play right now."

"Yeah, go play with Sandra," I said.

Sandra popped her head in the doorway.

"Yeah, come to me, Marcy-Warcy," Sandra crooned, covering Marcy with kisses. "How's my sweet baby girl?"

"Yuck," I said.

Momma shook her head at me. "You know, some-day you're going to wish you hadn't been so mean to your little sister."

I didn't say a word. I pretended I was reading. When they left, I tried to finish my history home-work. I didn't want to get into trouble with Ms. Canales again. I put my name and the date at the top of the page. I answered most of the questions, but I needed to look up one last thing on the computer. I left my homework on the desk and went into Sandra's room to use the computer.

When Marcy was born, her crib was in my parents' room. Her playpen and all her toys have always been in Sandra's room. Sandra doesn't seem to mind baby-sitting or having Marcy play in her room. But now that she's older, Marcy's crib is in my room and Daddy moved the computer from my room and into Sandra's.

"There's not enough space in your room for the baby's crib and dresser and your computer," Daddy explained. There was no use arguing.

Marcy changed everything when she arrived, in-cluding the way I had my room arranged.

I looked up the information I needed to finish my homework and printed it out. I went back to my room and finished my homework. I put the paper on top of my sneakers, which were on the floor by my bed. That way, I wouldn't forget it in the morning.

I got ready for bed. I closed my eyes, but couldn't fall asleep. I felt angry inside just thinking about everything that had happened that day. I put on the bedside lamp. Sometimes writing makes me feel better. I decided to write a letter to my best friend, Annette. She lives in Wichita, Kansas. We haven't seen each other since my family moved to Texas more than a year ago, but we e-mail and write letters. It was nice to have someone I could write to who understands me.

I pulled out my stationery and smoothed a sheet of paper. I am not the neatest person in the world. Sandra has that honor. So what if the paper is a little crinkled? Annette will understand. I searched for my pen, and found it under the bed inside a tennis shoe. I wrote:

Dear Annette,

I hope things are better for you than they are for me. I sure do miss you. I wish I could live with you and your parents and go to school in Kansas. I feel more left out at home than ever. I'm in trouble again for running my mouth and falling asleep in class. Marcy sleeps in my room now. Sometimes she wakes up in the middle of the night! I usually can get her to go back to sleep, but then I can't fall back asleep! I don't have my privacy anymore. And of course, just like Sandra, Marcy can do no wrong. It's always my fault, no matter what happens.

Well, so much for me. How are you doing? Do you still like middle school?

I miss you! No one can take your place. I'm still hanging out with Hannah. She's the girl that dresses crazy, but she's really nice. She can't take your place, though.

Your sister forever and your best friend,
Sharie

I folded the letter and put it into an envelope. I scrawled Annette's address on the front. I drew a weird-looking flower in the corner and then put little squiggles on the triangular flap. Maybe I'll color them tomorrow before I give Daddy the letter to mail.

I was still awake when Momma walked in carrying Marcy in her arms. I watched Momma gently put Marcy in her crib. Momma smiled at me as she patted Marcy on the back and covered her up.

"The little button is wiped out. She's been dancing. You should have seen her. I can't believe it's nine-thirty already."

"Why can't I stay up until ten?" I asked.

Momma gave me one of her famous sighs.

"Sharie, please. Give it a rest," Momma said. "You don't like to get up for school as it is. You need to go to bed early so you can get up early."

"Sure, Momma," I said, turning over in the bed so my back was to her.

"Good night, Sharie," Momma said as she turned off the light.

"'Night," I said. As soon as Momma left the

room, I rolled back over. Daddy used to come in and give me a good night kiss. Now, the only reason Momma and Daddy come into my room is to put Marcy in her crib. Everything revolves around the baby.

I'd finally fallen asleep when around two a.m. the Screech Doll started to cry. I got up and patted her on the back to lull her to sleep. She kept crying. I gave up and walked down the hall to my parents' room.

"Momma," I said as I pounded on their door. "The baby's crying again."

Marcy had been waking up a lot lately. At first, I tried to get her to go back to sleep without waking up my parents. But that was getting harder and harder to do. I decided to just let Momma or Daddy handle Marcy tonight. I was too tired.

Momma followed me down the hall and into my room. I climbed back into bed.

"Come on, little baby," Momma said, lifting Marcy out of her crib. "What's the matter? What do you want, huh?"

"Sharie! Sharie!" Marcy screamed. She reached

over and tried to grab me. I put my pillow over my head and rolled over.

"Me want Sharie! Me want Sharie!" Marcy yelled, loud enough to almost cave in the ceiling.

Marcy's middle of the night wake-up calls started three weeks ago. Now she wanted *me* to hold her — not Momma, not Daddy, not Sandra, just me. I don't want to hold her because then I can't sleep. Nobody will ever really understand how devious and cunning Marcy is toward me. Somehow she knows that no matter what she does to me, she'll never get into any trouble.

"Can you please hold her for a minute, Sharie?" Momma said. "I know you're tired and sleepy, but she wants you. Maybe if you rock her a little, she'll fall asleep."

I threw the pillow off my face and onto the floor. I swung my legs over the side of the bed and sat up. Momma handed her to me. Marcy instantly stopped crying. It figures!

Momma quietly walked into the hall. I moved to the rocking chair and rocked Marcy back and forth really fast, patting her on the back to lull her to sleep.

Then all of a sudden — *bam*! She hit her head on the back of the chair and started screaming.

"Sharie! What happened?" Momma said as she ran into my room and took Marcy from my arms.

"I didn't mean to hurt her," I pleaded. "Honest."

"Go to bed," Momma said, in one of the harshest tones I'd ever heard. "This is unbelievable."

"What on earth happened?" Daddy said, running into the room.

Marcy wailed even louder. Then Sandra came into my room, rubbing her eyes.

"Momma, is she alright? Why is she screaming like that?"

"Marcy hit her head against the rocking chair when Sharie was rocking her."

"It was an accident," I shouted above the noise.

In that split second, Marcy stopped crying. Now it sounded like I was shouting at my parents.

"I know good and well you aren't raising your voice," Daddy said.

"No, sir," I said quickly. "I was just trying to tell you what happened."

"We know what happened," Daddy said. "The baby hit her head while you were rocking her and now everyone is up trying to put her back to sleep."

I gave up trying to explain anything. I got back into bed. Momma put Marcy in her crib. She seemed to fall asleep instantly. I couldn't believe it.

"I have to get up before Sandra to catch the school bus," I said. "And this torture every night doesn't help."

"If you had been more careful, she wouldn't have hurt herself," Daddy said.

"It's late," Momma said. "Let's all go back to bed."

"But Momma," I began.

"Go to bed, all of you," Momma said as she walked down the hall.

I couldn't believe that Momma wasn't going to explain what had happened. It figures that Marcy would get me into trouble again!

Chapter Three

Sloppy Kisses and Stinky Diapers

I finally fell asleep, but not for long. For a moment, I thought I was outdoors and the rain was getting my face all wet. I rubbed my eyes and sat up face-to-face with Marcy. She was planting wet, sloppy kisses all over my face. Then, the alarm went off and nearly scared me to death.

"Stop kissing me," I said. I sniffed the air and realized that Marcy needed a diaper change. Yuck! I rolled out of the other side of the bed and ran down the hall. Marcy followed on my heels.

"Pick up me. Pick up me. Pwese! Pwese!"

"Stop following me," I said, slamming the bathroom door.

"Sharie!" Momma said. "Don't yell at the baby!"

I sighed and splashed cold water on my face. What a way to start the day — sloppy kisses and stinky diapers! I brushed my teeth and went into my room to get dressed for school.

"Sharie, please change the baby for me before you leave," Momma said as I was getting dressed.

Change her diaper, feed her, hold her, rock her. I was tired of taking care of Marcy.

"Okay," I said grumpily.

When I walked into my room, Marcy was sitting on the floor. She was busy chewing on something.

"What are you eating?"

Marcy took a wet glob of paper out of her mouth.

"Yuck," I said. I took the glob and threw it into the trash. I grabbed a diaper and the baby powder off the dresser.

"I'll be glad when you're old enough to use the bathroom," I said crossly. "I'm not putting your wet bottom on my bed, that's for sure. No way. And no one can make me, either."

I picked her up. Pieces of paper fell from her and

onto the floor. I picked one up, smoothed it out, and read part of my name. I could see the letters SHARI on the tiny scrap. What is this? Then it hit me. Marcy was eating my homework. I left my homework on my sneakers last night. She had taken it, torn it up, and eaten it.

"Momma!" I shouted. "The baby ate my homework."

Momma ran into the room. "What? What's the matter? Why is there blue stuff on her mouth? Sharie, did you leave your pen where she could get to it?"

"Marcy ate my homework! She took it off my sneakers."

"Come on, Sharie. Don't tell fibs. Did you really do your homework? Just tell the truth."

"I am telling the truth," I said, showing her the scrap of paper. "See, here's my proof."

"That? That's your proof that Marcy ate an entire sheet of paper? Come on, baby, come to Momma before your sister accuses you of something worse."

I handed the baby to Momma. "Take her. You never believe what I say. I did do my homework. I put

23

it on top of my sneakers. Then this morning I saw her eating something," I said.

"If you saw her eating paper, why didn't you stop her? Don't tell me you just watched her eat it and did nothing."

I started to say something to defend myself, but I didn't. "I've got to go or I'll be late. Will you write me an excuse?" I said.

"Nope. You're on your own. You need to be prepared for what happens when you don't take responsibility for your actions."

"It seems like I'm responsible for what happens to everyone around here," I mumbled as I stormed out of the room and out the door to the bus stop.

Normally any display of my temper brought Momma right behind me to scold me. But now that she has her precious baby she doesn't care about me anymore.

As soon as I got to class, I walked up to Ms. Canales's desk.

"I have something to tell you. I don't think you're going to believe it, but it's true," I said.

Ms. Canales pushed her glasses up on the bridge of her nose. "What is it now, Sharie? Did the dog eat your homework?"

The warning bell rang and the rest of the class filed in and took their seats.

"Not exactly," I said, reluctant to continue now. "I'll wait until later to talk to you about it," I said as I walked back to my seat.

I took out a sheet of paper and cupped my hand over it. I started to write a note to Ms. Canales.

Dear Ms. Canales,

Please excuse Sharie. She stayed up with the baby all last night. I'm sorry she doesn't have her homework today. It's all my fault. Please excuse her. She'll turn it in tomorrow.
Mrs. Angeline Johnson

I neatly folded the note. Then I put it in my pocket. I waited until Ms. Canales was alone at her desk before I walked back up to her.

"Here's my excuse, Ms. Canales," I said.

"Excuse for what?" Ms. Canales asked, pushing her glasses up.

"I don't have my homework," I said as I handed her the folded paper. I held my breath as she unfolded it. She held it up to read.

"Hmm," was all she said. Then she added, "Okay, Sharie. Take your seat, please."

Whew! I couldn't believe she didn't have anything else to say. All day long, she treated me very kindly.

The next day, she acted the same way. At lunch, I asked Hannah, "Can you believe how nice Ms. Canales is acting toward me?"

"I noticed that," Hannah said.

"She even told me that she's planning to give me a free period this afternoon to work on my play."

"You mean during class?" Hannah said. "No way."

"That's what she said — honest."

"Wow."

While we were talking, Caitlin Mullen walked over.

"Did I hear you say you're writing a new play?"

"That's right," I said.

"I'd like to try out for the lead," Caitlin said.

"I'm trying out for the lead," Hannah said.

I sighed. Hannah and Caitlin are always competing with each other. I hate being in the middle.

When I first moved to Austin, Caitlin didn't seem to like me at all. Then I wrote a play and let her share the lead with Hannah and we became friends. Last year, Hannah, Caitlin, and I became even closer after our fifth-grade teacher, Mrs. Bailes, gave us a homework assignment over the holidays. That's when I learned how lonely Caitlin really was and how sweet she could be. She celebrated Kwanzaa with my family, and we both learned a lot about each other.

"I don't know who will be the lead character yet. I sort of have an athletic girl in mind."

"I can play tennis," Caitlin said quickly.

"I think she means athletic-looking," Hannah said.

"I don't think I was talking to you," Caitlin said.

Caitlin's other friends, Anysa Bailey and Karly Norris, stopped by.

"Come on, Caitlin," Anysa said. "We have to stop by the office, remember?"

Anysa smiled at me. I knew what she was trying to do. She wanted to get Caitlin away from Hannah. For some reason, Hannah and Caitlin are always trying to upstage each other.

"Listen Caitlin, when I figure everything out, I'll let you know," I said.

Hannah said, "What about me? I'm your best friend."

I whispered, "You'll be the first to know."

Hannah repeated loudly, "You're right! I'll be the first to know. After all, I'm your best friend."

That's how it is between the two of them, constant friction. Hannah Lowenstein is the most unpopular girl in the sixth grade. It must be tough, because she was the most unpopular girl in the fifth grade, too. Even being one of the stars of last year's play didn't help very much. All the kids think she's weird. I try to help her steer clear of Caitlin. You can't constantly say smart-mouthed things to the most popular girl and survive.

Hannah is stubborn. She feels that just because Caitlin is rich, pretty, and talented doesn't give her a

reason to act like such a snob. I've told Hannah about how nice Caitlin can be, but that doesn't help. She still insists that Caitlin doesn't have to be the way she is and that's that.

Sometimes I get tired of defending Hannah. People are always asking me, "What's wrong with Hannah? Why does she wear those crazy outfits?"

"She likes to be different," I always say.

At that point, I usually walk away. Sometimes, I suggest to Hannah that she should tone down her outfits. But then she just looks at me from head to toe. I get the point. Like right now, I have a big ink stain on my pants because I'm always sticking my ink pens in my pockets. I look terrible. Do I care? No.

I'm not like Sandra, my sister who is two years older. All she thinks about is clothes, clothes, and more clothes. I have better things to think about, like my new play.

"Stop daydreaming," Hannah said. "We're going to be late for class."

I was in class only a few minutes when Ms. Canales came up to me.

"How are you feeling?" she asked.

It was the third time today she'd asked me that.

"I'm fine," I said, taking out my history book.

"Don't forget that during the last period you can work on your play."

I stared at her. It must be be-nice-to-Sharie week or something.

As soon as the last period started, I put away my books and pulled out my play. The lead character in my play would be a lot like me. She's constantly criticized by her parents and her teacher because she speaks without thinking. She loves playwriting and baseball, just like I do. She has a perfect older sister and a bratty baby sister, too. She's not exactly like me, though, because my new character is pretty and popular in school. She never forgets her homework, loves fashion, and she always looks neat and clean. That is *not* a description that fits me.

I bit my pencil as I reread what I had written. Hmm. She has to have some flaws. Maybe she can rush into things. Or maybe she can be really pushy when she wants her way. She also needs a major obstacle to overcome. Maybe she can find herself suddenly unpopular. Yes, that's it! I can write about that. I definitely know about being unpopular.

Hannah could play the lead part. She's not very popular. She also knows how my life is with Sandra and Marcy, and how terrible that can be. She can rush into things and be pushy, too. Wait — that's it! I'll make the character more like Hannah. And her goal will be to overcome her character flaws to become popular. I made some changes to the script. I was almost finished when the bell rang. I started putting things into my bookbag.

"I have some good news for you," I said to Hannah.

"What is it? Tell me, tell me, tell me," she said, rushing to gather her things. Hannah is always in a hurry.

"Just wait a sec. I'll tell you when we get to our lockers."

I knew she'd be pleased to have the lead in my play. The part was perfect for her.

Then Ms. Canales called me. "Excuse me, Sharie. Could I see you before you leave?"

I gave Hannah a look. What now?

Hannah shrugged her shoulders and walked out the door.

Ms. Canales was holding my homework excuse.

I squirmed. I was busted! Ms. Canales would drag me to the principal's office and then call my parents. I was doomed.

Chapter Four

◎◎◎◎◎◎◎◎◎◎◎◎◎◎◎◎◎◎◎◎◎◎◎◎◎◎

The Baby Ate My Homework

I was a goner. My palms felt like I'd dipped them in a bucket of ice-cold water.

Ms. Canales looked at the note again. She removed her glasses.

"I'm sorry you're having such a rough time at home, Sharie. Believe me, we're going to help you."

I didn't know what to say. *They* were going to help me? Who were *they*? And what were they going to help me do? I was about to ask Ms. Canales what she meant when another woman I'd never seen before entered the room.

Ms. Canales said, "Sharie, this is someone who

can help you. Grace Compton, this is Sharie Johnson, the young lady I spoke to you about."

I looked from Ms. Canales to Mrs. Compton. Who was she?

She stuck out her hand. "Hello, Sharie, nice to meet you," she said. "Would you mind if we talked for a few minutes?"

I froze. Was she the police? Could I get in trouble with the law for writing a fake excuse? Would she take me to jail? I could feel the sweat dripping off my forehead. I wanted to confess, but instead I silently sat down across from her as she squeezed into a desk. Her stomach pushed up against the desktop. I wanted to ask if she would be more comfortable in a chair, but before I could say anything, Ms. Canales passed my note to her. I closed my eyes. *Oh, no, what had I done now?* My parents would ground me for lying and forging Momma's name.

"Sharie, I have a few questions and then you can go. How do you get along with your mother?"

I stared at her. "Fine. Why?" I asked.

"We suspect that you wrote this note. I notice that you say you've been taking care of your baby sister all night," Mrs. Compton said.

"Well, sometimes I do," I said.

"What about your father?"

"What about him?" I asked.

Mrs. Compton cleared her throat. "How do you get along with him?"

"We get along fine," I said. "Why?"

"I'm just wondering why he doesn't help with your baby sister."

"He helps take care of her," I said. "We all take care of her."

Now I got it. Ms. Canales and Mrs. Compton thought Momma and Daddy were being mean to me. They thought that my parents were making me take care of Marcy all night long. Oh, no! My parents would be so disappointed if they thought that someone felt they were bad parents. That would hurt them. This would be worse than going to jail. I needed to confess.

"Wait a minute," I said. "I'm sorry, Ms. Canales. What I wrote about my baby sister Marcy sometimes keeping me awake is true. But the reason I don't have my homework is because the baby ate it."

"Your baby sister ate your homework?" Mrs. Compton asked as she glanced over at Ms. Canales.

"Yes," I said.

"So you aren't being kept awake by your baby sister?" asked Ms. Canales.

"No, I am. You see, Marcy sleeps in my room and she's always waking up in the middle of the night. Momma or Daddy always comes and gets her when she wakes up. Sometimes, my sister Sandra gets up to help with her, too. But most of the time, I'm the only one she'll let put her back to sleep."

"So, you're not getting enough sleep at night," Ms. Canales said. "That's why you keep nodding off in class."

"But that's not my parents' fault," I said. "I don't know why the baby always wants me to rock her to sleep. Everyone else has tried to do it, but she won't let anyone else but me put her back to sleep."

"Oh, I think I understand the problem now," Mrs. Compton said.

"And what's this about the baby eating your homework?" Ms. Canales asked.

"See, this morning I saw her eating something, but I was too late to stop her," I explained. "It turned out that she was eating my homework. I wanted to tell you, but I thought that you wouldn't believe me. That's why I wrote the note. Then I signed my momma's name to it."

"Sharie is a smart sixth grader," Ms. Canales said, "but sometimes she does things without thinking."

"What were you thinking when you wrote this note?" Mrs. Compton asked.

I could see they both were very frustrated. Now I understood why Ms. Canales had been so nice to me. She thought my family was treating me badly. She thought my parents made me babysit Marcy all night long when I should be sleeping.

"Please don't tell my parents," I said, tears welling up in my eyes. I was really going to get it now.

"I have to talk to them, Sharie," Ms. Canales said. "You've been sleeping in class and you lied to me.

Your parents are lovely. I should have known better than to drag you into this, Grace."

"No problem," Mrs. Compton said. It turned out Mrs. Compton was a personal friend of Ms. Canales and a counselor. It seemed that Ms. Canales wanted to get her professional opinion about my family.

"Sharie, you need to learn that lying only creates more problems. I think your parents will be very disappointed," she said.

"I said I was sorry," I said. "I really am."

"You should be," Ms. Canales said. "Tonight, I want you to sit down and talk with your parents. Together you need to come up with a solution to your problems at home. I'll speak with them soon, either on the phone or at the parent-teacher conference that's coming up. Make sure they come. You can go now."

"Are you going to call them today?" I asked her.

"I will talk to them when I'm ready," Ms. Canales said.

Ms. Canales was not about to change her mind. I

left the room with my head hanging low. I was doomed.

Hannah was waiting for me at her locker. "What happened? Have you been crying?"

I told her everything. I couldn't keep it to myself.

"Why did you do that?" she asked me.

"I don't know," I said, and I didn't. I didn't have a clue why I wrote the note and forged my mother's name. I was doing so many crazy things I didn't even feel like myself anymore. Instead of improving, I was going backward at school. Lying always got me into trouble, but I never seemed to learn from my mistakes.

Mrs. Lowenstein came to pick us up. I didn't say very much on the way home. I just stared out of the window.

As soon as I got home, I ran upstairs and took a nap. I didn't want to think about what had happened at school that day. I slept for about an hour. Then I got up and worked on my play. Writing always made me feel better.

I rewrote everything. The main character needed

to be more interesting. I decided to turn her into a pushy, weird dressing, know-it-all who was the most unpopular girl in school. She finally becomes friends with a girl who feels bad for her. And her new friend learns that she's really a great person, after all. I didn't stop writing until Momma knocked on my door.

"Will you change the baby for me?" Momma asked, bringing Marcy into my room. "I need to finish cooking dinner and Sandra is setting the table."

I picked Marcy up. Then I felt a wet stain on my shirt.

"Oh, gross!" I said as I put Marcy on the changing table. I grabbed a wet wipe and scrubbed my shirt.

"Momma, she's soaking wet," I said. Yuck! I scrubbed my shirt with another wet wipe.

I tried to change Marcy, but she kept grabbing my hair and pulling it out of the ponytail holder. I caught a glimpse of myself in the mirror. I looked like a clown. My hair was standing up on my head. Marcy pointed at me and laughed. I tickled Marcy with my hair and she giggled loudly. I like making her laugh.

41

I carried Marcy into the dining room on my hip. I fastened her into her high chair. She immediately started to wail like a fire engine.

"Sharie, up. Sharie, up," she cried, holding her arms stretched out toward me.

Momma walked in the room. "She's so sweet. She wants you to hold her, Sharie."

"Yeah, well I don't want to hold her," I said grumpily. "She plays with my food when I'm trying to eat. I hate for anyone to touch my food."

Sandra came in and cooed to Marcy.

"Come on, Peaches, your big sister will hold you," she said, unsnapping the straps. She picked up Marcy and sat down, showering her with kisses. Marcy squealed with delight. Then she pushed Sandra away, ran to me, and grabbed my legs tightly. I couldn't move.

I picked her up. It was no use. Marcy loved me no matter what. I didn't deserve it, but she loved me anyway. I hugged her and swung her around and around. She squealed and laughed. Momma and Sandra laughed at us, too. I started feeling a little better.

That night at dinner, Daddy asked, "How's school going, girls?"

Sandra bragged on and on about her duties as Class President. She was beginning to put some of her campaign pledges into action. She acted as though she had been elected to Congress.

I was so bored that I stabbed one green bean after another until I had about ten stuck on my fork. Then the phone rang. I stopped breathing. Was that Ms. Canales? If so, my goose was cooked.

Momma got up to answer it. Usually Sandra raced to the phone, but she had Marcy on her lap.

Momma didn't look any different when she returned. It wasn't Ms. Canales.

"That was Hannah's mother," Momma said. "She wanted to tell me that Hannah won't be coming over on Friday night."

Hannah usually spent Friday nights with us if her mother had to travel out-of-town on business. This had been going on ever since Hannah and I became friends. We had lots of fun on those Friday nights. We put on plays. I usually wrote the scripts. Then Hannah made the sets out of bedsheets, cardboard, or whatever she found in my room. We both acted in them.

I was disappointed. I enjoyed Hannah's visits.

"Is her mother going out of town?" I asked.

"I don't know," Momma said. "She just wanted to tell me that Hannah was spending the night somewhere else."

"What?" I said. "Where? Is she staying with her grandmother?"

"I don't know," Momma said. "I didn't ask."

Something was going on with Hannah. I just knew it. This was turning out to be one of the worst days of my life.

"May I be excused?" I said.

Daddy sat back in his chair. He looked concerned. I love sweets, especially chocolate pudding. I only skip dessert if I'm sick.

"You don't want dessert?" he asked. "What's wrong?"

"I'm just tired," I said. "I'm going to bed early."

"Go on then," Daddy said.

"Good night," everyone said.

"Sharie, kissy!" Marcy said.

I kissed Marcy quickly. I didn't notice that she had food all over her face. Yuck! I wiped my mouth with my hand. Marcy smiled at me happily and blew me a kiss. I taught her how to do that. I heard Momma say to Daddy as I went upstairs, "I don't understand what has gotten into Sharie lately."

I climbed into bed, but I couldn't fall asleep. I kept thinking about everything that happened. I wanted to know where Hannah was spending the night. It wasn't like her not to tell me if she was going to her grandma's for the weekend.

I decided I wouldn't be able to sleep until I called Hannah. I quickly dialed her number.

"Hey," Hannah said. "I'm glad you called. Did you tell your folks about what happened today?"

"No. I don't know when I'll tell them. Maybe Ms. Canales won't squeal on me."

"Yeah, and maybe she won't give us a final exam, either. And maybe she will give everyone in our class an A plus. And maybe . . ."

"Okay! Okay, enough! Anyway, why didn't you tell me you were going to your grandma's this weekend? I thought we were going to work on my new play together. I wrote a part just for you."

There was silence on the other end of the phone.

"Did you hear me?" I asked her.

"Yeah, I heard you. It's just that, well, I'm not going to my grandma's."

"Then where are you staying? Don't tell me your mother is going to let you stay alone. I wouldn't believe that."

"You know better than that," Hannah said laughing.

"Is your mom going out of town?"

"Yes," Hannah said quietly. Too quietly — something was up.

"So, if she's going out of town, and you're not going to your grandma's, and you're not staying by yourself, and you're not coming over here — then what?

Hannah cleared her throat. That was one of her stalling tactics that annoyed me.

"Tell me — where are you staying?"

I was her only friend. Everyone at school either thought she was crazy or too stuck-up to hang out with.

"I'm spending the night with Taylor Parker," she said, sighing like a burden had been lifted from her shoulders.

"Taylor? Who's that? One of your cousins?"

"No, remember she was the girl that I met at my mother's conference? I told you all about her."

"Oh, I'd forgotten all about that."

"Remember, I told you I went with my mother to a conference and Taylor was there with her mom? Well, it turns out that Taylor's mother knows my mother," Hannah explained. "Taylor and I started talking and hit it off. She's transferring to our school in a few days. She's a singer and an actress in California. Now that the filming for her television series is over, she's moving with her family to Austin."

I was stunned. Hannah Lowenstein had a new friend. Not a wacky friend, but a television star. And she was moving to our school. Ever since I came to

Austin it had just been Hannah and me. Sure, I hung out with Caitlin and her friends sometimes, but I never abandoned Hannah. Even when Caitlin didn't want Hannah hanging around, I usually invited her to come with us. Maybe not every time, but most of the time.

"Are you there?" Hannah asked. "You aren't upset, are you?"

"Of course not," I said. "Well, okay. I've got to go now."

I was upset, but I didn't want Hannah to know it. It seemed like I was lying all the time now. Why didn't I just tell her how I felt? Maybe I was a little, tiny-bit jealous.

It was clear to me now. The only true friend I had here in Austin was Hannah. And she was moving on and making a new friend. I would be alone.

Chapter Five

Trouble, Trouble, and More Trouble!

I quickly got off the phone. I had nothing left to say to Hannah. I felt like crying.

I went to my room and got back into bed. A little later, Momma and Marcy came into the room. Momma put Marcy into her crib.

" 'Night, girls," Momma said. She kissed us both good night and went out the door.

Seconds later, Marcy was standing up in her crib.

"Spit," Marcy said. "Spit."

I laughed. Marcy thinks "spit" means "kiss." It's because every time she wants to kiss me I say, "Please don't spit on me." Now she thinks spit means kiss. I gave her a big kiss and laid her down in her crib. At least someone loves me.

That night, I dreamed that my play was a huge success and I instantly became the most popular girl in Bailey Middle School. Caitlin Mullen, Anysa Bailey, Karly Norris, Hannah Lowenstein, and even Taylor Parker were following me around like puppies. In my dream, they all kept begging me to be their best friend. I told them I would let them each be my best friend for a week at a time, just to be fair.

When I woke up, I stayed in bed a minute thinking about everything that had happened to me. I was in trouble at home and at school. And now, I was in trouble with my only friend. I kicked off the covers and got up to get ready for school.

I could tell that Ms. Canales was still concerned about me. After school, she cornered me just as I was about to sprint out the door.

"Hold on a minute, Sharie," she said. "I want you to know that I've decided to wait until the parent-teacher conference to discuss your behavior with your parents. I want to give you plenty of time to talk with them and try to work out some sort of solution for your problems. I also want you to redo the homework assignment that your sister, uh, ate. You can turn it in tomorrow."

"Okay, Ms. Canales," I said.

I left the room as quickly as I could without running. Hannah was waiting for me at my locker.

"What did she say this time?" Hannah asked.

I didn't feel like telling her. "Nothing. She didn't say anything."

"Ms. Canales didn't say anything to you?"

"That's what I said." I yanked open my locker door. It slammed hard against the locker next to it. I took out my books and put them in my backpack.

Ms. Canales came down the hall. She stopped and patted me on the back.

"Get a good night's sleep. I look forward to seeing your homework tomorrow, okay?"

"Okay," I said.

"What was that about?" Hannah asked.

"Nothing," I said.

"Why are you taking your books? We don't have any homework tonight," Hannah said.

"Yeah, well, I do."

"Are you in some kind of trouble?"

"Hannah, I don't want to talk about it," I said.

"Okay, fine!" Hannah said. "Come on. My mom's here to pick us up."

I got in the car and we rode home in silence. Hannah's mother talked the entire way about her friend, Caroline Parker. She's Taylor's mother. Mrs. Parker is a famous children's book author. Hannah went on and on about Taylor Parker and her television series.

I didn't want to hear it. Mrs. Lowenstein and Hannah had friends moving to Austin. So what? The Parkers are a famous and talented family. So what? All I wanted to do was to go home and get away from everyone. I was having a terrible day.

When I got home, Momma said, "Sharie, I need to pick Sandra up from school. She's bringing a big project home and she can't ride the bus. Will you watch Marcy for five minutes? I'll be right back."

I wanted to say no. I was tired. I had had a bad day and I didn't feel like watching Marcy. But I said that I would babysit.

I carried Marcy into my room and sat her down on the floor.

"Sit right there, Marcy. Don't touch anything. Here's your stuffed elephant."

Marcy grabbed the elephant and happily chewed on its ear.

I walked into the bathroom. I got a towel and washed my face. I stared at myself in the mirror. How was I going to tell Momma and Daddy that I'd been sleeping in class? What would they say when they found out I wrote a note and signed Momma's name? I was in big trouble. I needed a solution to my problems — and fast.

When I walked out of the bathroom, Marcy was still playing with her elephant.

"Spit," Marcy said holding up the elephant. She hugged it and gave it a big, wet kiss.

"That's a good girl," I said. "Play with your elephant."

I decided to use the computer for a little while. Momma and Sandra wouldn't be home for a few more minutes. That meant I could play until Sandra stormed into her room and demanded that I get out of there. I turned it on and it wasn't long before I was winning the war against the space creatures. Suddenly, I heard the front door slam. Momma and Sandra were home.

"We're home, Sharie," Momma called.

"Okay," I said. I was beating my all-time best score. I wasn't about to stop playing. I didn't care what Sandra said.

I was lost in the game when I heard Sandra yelling. I turned off the computer and ran into the hall. Sandra was holding Marcy on her hip.

"Why was Marcy alone in your room?" Sandra demanded.

"I just left her alone for a minute," I said. "Is she okay?"

"Yes, but your room isn't!" Sandra said. "She was tearing up everything in there."

I ran past Sandra and into my room. There was a

pile of ripped paper on the floor. I smoothed out one of the scraps. It took a minute before I realized what it was.

"Momma!" I screamed.

Momma rushed into my room. She said, "What's the matter, Sharie? Are you alright?"

"No, look!" I shouted. "Just look what Marcy did!"

Momma looked down at the pile. "What is it?"

"They're my letters from Annette, Momma," I said, tears streaming down my face. "I've been saving them ever since we moved here from Kansas." I held up the empty letter box.

"My goodness, Sharie!" Momma said. "You scared me to death. I thought you were hurt."

"But, Momma," I said. "Marcy ripped up all my letters."

"Well, if you'd put your things up high like I've asked you to, this wouldn't have happened. Marcy doesn't understand that the letters are valuable to you. You have to take responsibility for your things and put them in a place where she can't get them."

I couldn't believe that she was taking Marcy's side.

"You should have been watching her. You must have seen her with the letters," Momma said. "Why didn't you take them away from her?"

"When I came home, Marcy was in Sharie's room all by herself," Sandra said. She handed Marcy to Momma and then went to her room.

"Sharie!" Momma said. "Didn't I ask you to watch her? Don't you know she could hurt herself if no one is paying attention to her?"

"I just left her alone for a minute," I said.

"Your sister is still a baby," Momma said. "I wasn't gone that long. Couldn't you just be responsible for her for a few minutes?"

"I'm tired of babysitting Marcy," I said stubbornly. "I'm tired of changing her. I'm tired of her keeping me up at night. I'm tired of her tearing up my things. I'm tired of her — period."

"That's enough," Momma said. "I asked if you would mind babysitting Marcy and you said you didn't. If you had told me that you didn't want to babysit, I would have taken Marcy with me. I don't appreciate the things you said about your sister and I don't appreciate your attitude. I'm taking some of your privileges away for two weeks. No phone calls or computer games until you start taking responsibility for your things. This family works together. When I ask you to babysit Marcy, I expect you to watch her. I'm not asking too much of you, am I?"

"No, ma'am," I said, dropping my head. I felt torn up inside. Momma was right.

"I have to finish cooking dinner," Momma said. "Sandra, will you watch Marcy for me?"

"Of course, Momma," Sandra said. "Come on, baby," Sandra said, taking Marcy out of Momma's arms.

I sat on the floor and tried to sort through all the tiny pieces of ripped paper. I kept all my letters in a box under my bed so I could read them before I fell asleep. Why should I have to put them way up on a shelf? It's my room, I should be able to keep my personal things where I want.

It was no use. The letters were ruined. I cried as I picked up the pieces of paper and threw them into the trash. My letters were gone forever.

After dinner, Daddy stopped me before I went upstairs. I tried not to look at him. I could tell that he was upset.

"Sharie, your mother tells me that you've been having a hard day. I hope you're planning to get your act together real soon."

For my daddy, that was a short lecture. I didn't want to blow it by saying anything smart-mouthed. No need to get in more trouble.

"Yes, sir, I will," I said, and quickly ran upstairs to my bedroom. When I'm in there, I can get away from my troubles. I lay on the bed and closed my eyes. A few seconds later, I heard the patter of Marcy's feet. The next thing I knew she was in the room, staring at me.

"What are you looking at?" I said crossly.

Before Marcy was born, life was a lot better for me. I was bringing up my grades and I had made new friends. Now, it seemed like I was in trouble all the time. I glared at her and stuck out my tongue.

She giggled with laughter. She stuck out her tongue, too.

"Spit, Sharie," Marcy said. "Spit."

I had to laugh. I couldn't stay mad at Marcy. She was too funny. I gave her a big kiss and tickled her. I needed to figure out a way to talk to Momma and Daddy about my problems without making it seem as though I didn't love my baby sister. Because I had to admit it, I really do.

Chapter Six

The New Girl

Ms. Canales was explaining an assignment when someone knocked loudly on the classroom door.

Ms. Canales opened the door and went into the hall. When she returned, she was not alone.

"Class, this is Taylor Parker," Ms. Canales said with a smile. "She's our new student."

Hannah smiled and waved at Taylor. She motioned toward the empty desk beside her. Taylor smiled shyly and waved back.

Ms. Canales continued, "Taylor has just moved from Los Angeles to join our class. Isn't that wonderful?"

I didn't remember getting this type of introduction when I moved to Austin. In fact, I couldn't remember Ms. Canales introducing any new student this way. What was the big deal about Taylor Parker?

Tommy Wall said, "Hey, wait a minute, Ms. Canales! I know who she is! She's famous, isn't she?"

Taylor smiled at him.

"Taylor, would you like to answer him?" Ms. Canales asked.

Before Taylor could say anything, Caitlin raised her hand.

Ms. Canales said, "Yes, Caitlin? What is it?"

"Is she the girl from the *America's Most Talented Kid* contest?"

A buzz filled the class.

"Yes, she is," Ms. Canales said, almost gleaming. "Taylor won the contest last year. She was also on the television show *Middle School Stories*. Did any of you see that?"

"I saw that show," Tommy said. "Wow! You were great!"

"Thank you," Taylor said softly.

Everyone looked impressed. I just stared out the window. Taylor was famous — big deal! I hated to admit it, but I was jealous. I couldn't believe I was feeling this way. Most of the time I would be excited to meet someone as famous as Taylor.

"Okay, class, settle down. Taylor, you can sit at the empty desk by Hannah Lowenstein. I understand you already know each other. Now let's get back to work."

Ms. Canales continued explaining the assignment. Everyone in the class kept sneaking peeks at our new celebrity. She seemed down-to-earth and normal. What if Taylor and I became best friends? Suddenly, I'd be one of the most popular girls in school.

As I was daydreaming, I missed hearing Ms. Canales's announcement.

She decided to choose someone to show Taylor around the school for the next week. Hannah raised her hand to be her partner. As a matter of fact, everyone seemed to have their hand up to show Taylor around, except for me. Ms. Canales picked Hannah!

I couldn't believe it. Hannah usually never raises

her hand for things like that. No one ever picks her, so most of the time I do, or she raises her hand and asks to partner with me.

"Can we start a list of people who want to be Taylor's partner?" Caitlin asked. "Maybe she could have a new partner every day?"

"Whoever heard of a waiting list to be someone's partner?" I said. "That's just silly."

"There's a first time for everything, Sharie," Ms. Canales said. "I'm glad the class is making our new student feel so welcome. Caitlin, since you brought up the idea, I'll let you be first on the list. Who's next?"

Hands shot up. I couldn't believe it! My school year was going from bad to worse. I'm in trouble with Ms. Canales for writing the fake note, I'm grounded with my parents because of Marcy, and now, Hannah seems to like Taylor better than she likes me!

After school, I walked to my locker to meet Hannah. Sometimes, her mom picks us up and sometimes Hannah rides the bus home with me.

Hannah was rearranging her books. She wouldn't look at me, so I could tell that something was up.

"Are you going straight home?" Hannah asked.

"No, I'm going to Mars. Where else would I go?" I said crossly. I was still upset that she was going to be Taylor's partner.

"Well, I thought maybe you could catch the bus today," Hannah said. "I have something to do after school."

I stared at her. Hannah always includes me in her after-school plans. Everything had changed between us in just one day.

"Sure, no problem. I can catch the bus. What's up? Your mother's not picking you up today?"

"No, she's not," Hannah said.

"How are you getting home?" I asked.

"I've got another ride," Hannah said.

"With who?" I asked.

I didn't have to wait very long for an answer. Taylor opened up the door and waved at Hannah.

"Come on, Hannah," Taylor said. "My mom is here."

"Okay," Hannah called back. "Sorry, Sharie. I've got to run. See you later."

"See you," I said.

And just like that my best friend, the most unpopular girl in the sixth grade, was gone. I stood there for a minute thinking about what had just happened. Hannah had brushed me off to go home with Taylor. Well, too bad. We'll see tomorrow if this Taylor will still want to hang out with the most unpopular kid here. I doubt it.

I checked my watch. The bus would be leaving in a few minutes. I pretended I was looking for something in my locker. Maybe by the time I went outside, Hannah and Taylor would be gone. I didn't feel up to seeing Taylor drive off with my best friend.

When I finally stepped outside, I saw Hannah and Taylor surrounded by a bunch of kids near a big, fancy, luxury car. The windows were tinted black, so I couldn't see inside the car. It looked like something a movie star would ride in.

Some of the kids were getting Taylor's autograph. Everyone seemed to listen intently to every word she said.

"I couldn't believe all the cool stuff Hannah

knows," Taylor said. "I was like 'Wow, this girl has got to be my friend.' I also love the way she dresses. It's so cool."

Caitlin was standing next to Taylor and said, "Yes, we love the way Hannah dresses, too. It's so unique."

Hannah looked as stunned as I felt. I couldn't believe it. Caitlin had always made fun of the way Hannah dresses.

As I walked past them, Hannah didn't even wave at me. In all fairness, maybe she didn't see me. The crowd around them was so big. I climbed on the bus and looked out the window at Hannah and Taylor. This was turning out to be one of the worst weeks of my life.

As soon as I got home, I went upstairs and did my homework. Momma stopped by my room and asked me if I was feeling ill. I shook my head. I didn't want to tell her that I'd never felt so miserable before in my life.

Caitlin, Anysa, and Karly are my friends, but Hannah and I are best friends. At least I thought we were.

Sandra was on the computer, so I decided to watch television. It was just my luck that a repeat of the *America's Most Talented Kid* contest was on. There she was, Taylor Blayne (Tweetie) Parker singing in the final competition. I hated to admit it, but she was great. I mean, the girl can really sing. Taylor was declared the winner and the host gave her a check for $100,000.

After the show was over, I watched Taylor's interview. She seemed really nice. It was while watching the interview that I found out she is a straight-A student. How is it that people like her and Sandra exist? They have looks, brains, and personality.

As the days passed, my life got worse. Hannah had no time for me. She spent every free minute with Taylor. Then Ms. Canales mentioned the parent-teacher conference. She reminded me to talk to my parents and work out a solution before she met with them.

To make matters worse, every single boy and girl in our school constantly drools over Taylor. Since Taylor and Hannah are such good friends, everyone hangs around Hannah now, too. Hannah doesn't seem to have time for me anymore. Last week, I had given her a copy of my unfinished play, but she hadn't told me what she thought about it. What was the point? She probably wouldn't want to be in it now that Taylor was her new best friend.

I could barely stand to hear Taylor talk. Every day, she had something interesting or funny to say. I wish she wasn't so smart. Every time Ms. Canales asked a question, Taylor's hand flew up in the air. Honestly, how could any one person know so much about every single topic? I was jealous, and I hated feeling like that.

Plus, Ms. Canales kept asking me how things were going at home. I told her everything was okay, but she knows that I still fall asleep sometimes in class. Marcy has a cold and she's keeping everyone in the house awake all night. We're so tired that we usually eat dinner and go right to bed. Of course, Marcy wakes us all up in the middle of the night. And she only lets me rock her to sleep. I don't know what we're going to do.

The day before the parent-teacher conference, I

came up with a plan to keep Momma and Daddy from talking to Ms. Canales. We were eating dinner when I said, "You know what, I think tomorrow is going to be one of the worst parent-teacher conferences in history. They're planning some long, drawn-out program before you even get to talk to anyone. And Ms. Canales can really talk a lot. I bet if you go at seven p.m. you won't get back until midnight. I also heard that the people at Bailey Middle School don't like it when babies come to the meetings, so we won't be able to take Marcy.

The one thing Daddy hated was long, drawn-out meetings. And Momma always had a hard time finding a babysitter for Marcy.

"We weren't born yesterday, Sharie," Daddy said. "We're going to the parent-teacher conference."

I gave up.

The next day I made one final plea to Ms. Canales. "I haven't talked back in over a week. I have completed all my homework. So please, don't tell my parents."

Ms. Canales said, "Sharie, you've continued to daydream instead of pay attention in class."

I walked back to my desk in silence. Ms. Canales was right. My mind had been wandering. I didn't know what to do about losing my best friend. I'd given her my revised play and so far, she refused to tell me what she thought about it. She wasn't even begging me for the lead part. Hannah just didn't seem to have time for me anymore. Every day, as soon as the last bell rang, Hannah and Taylor were surrounded by kids who wanted Taylor's autograph. Then Hannah usually went over to Taylor's house. Taylor had invited me twice to go with them after school, but I didn't want to hang out with her. Not after she took my best friend away from me.

Today was no different. On the way to the cafeteria I asked Hannah, "Do you want to sit with me at lunch?"

"Sure, but can Taylor sit with us, too?"

I wanted to say no way, but I said, "I don't care."

"Great," Hannah said. "I'll tell her. Taylor is really a nice person."

"Yeah, okay. I never said she wasn't."

Hannah said, "You don't have to say it. You're

constantly putting her down. It's not her fault she's smart and popular."

"Like it's not your fault that you were unpopular, right?" I didn't mean to say it. It just popped out.

"That was very mean," Hannah said.

"I'm sorry," I said. "I take it back."

"You already said it. It's just like the way you talk about me in your play."

"Oh," I said. "So you finally read it?"

"I read it alright," Hannah said. "You decided I was right for the part because it described me. I used to think you were my best friend. But if that's how you see me, you were just being nice because you felt sorry for me."

"That's not true," I said. But deep down I knew she was right. I wrote the part because that's how I saw her as a person.

"See, I don't mind if people think I'm different and that I dress weird. I don't even mind if they think I'm a know-it-all. But I do mind if someone is only my friend because they feel sorry for me."

"You've got it all wrong," I said.

"I don't think so," Hannah said. "After I read that play, I felt like I didn't really know you, after all."

I didn't know what to say. I never thought Hannah would be upset about my play. As soon as we walked into the cafeteria, Caitlin asked Hannah, "Where are you and Taylor sitting?"

"You can sit with me, Caitlin," I said.

"Are you sitting with Hannah and Taylor?" she asked.

"No, I'm sitting with myself," I said, hearing the sarcasm in my voice.

"Look, both of you can sit with us, if you want to," Hannah said.

"No, thanks," I said. "I'll sit over there."

I got in line to get my lunch. Taylor, Hannah, Caitlin, Anysa, and Karly laughed and talked as they went down the line. They all sat together. I sat by myself. I felt really sad.

I watched kids stopping by to talk to Taylor or ask her for an autograph. She smiled at everyone. I like making new friends and Taylor seemed like a nice person. But I just felt so jealous that Hannah seemed to like her more than she liked me. I had never been jealous of anyone before. It was a bad feeling.

I heard someone behind me say that the principal had asked Taylor to sing at the parent-teacher conferences that night. I sighed. I'd forgotten all about that. Once Momma and Daddy talked to Ms. Canales, my life would go from bad to worse.

When I got home from school, I tried one last time to talk my parents into not going. It didn't work. Sandra had a music lesson so Marcy would have to come to the conference with us. That meant I would have to hold her while they went in to talk with Ms. Canales.

Momma said, "Are you going to be okay helping us with the baby?"

"Yes, ma'am," I said.

"Are you sure?" Momma asked again. She always asked me twice about taking care of Marcy because of the problem we had last time.

"I don't mind," I said. "Honest."

We dropped Sandra off at her music lesson. She's working on a duet with her friend Jennie.

" 'Bye," Sandra said. "See you later! Have fun at the conference."

As if that's possible! I thought to myself. Marcy sang and clapped her hands all the way to the school. It was driving me crazy. I kept trying to think of a way to explain to Momma and Daddy about writing the note. I couldn't think of anything. I felt sick.

When we walked into the auditorium I could barely breathe. Ms. Canales was watching the door as though she was waiting for us. I tried to hide behind Daddy, but it was no use. She spotted me and walked over to my parents. I was doomed.

Chapter Seven

~~~~~~

The Parent-Teacher Conference

Ms. Canales came up and shook both my parents' hands.

"Hello, Sharie. Hello, Mr. and Mrs. Johnson," Ms. Canales said with a smile. "I'm looking forward to our meeting."

"Hi," I said quickly. "I'm going to take Marcy and sit down before all the seats are taken."

"That's a good idea," Momma said. She turned back to talk with Ms. Canales. I couldn't hear what Ms. Canales was saying. It's times like these that I wish I had super hearing. Momma and Daddy had their backs to me, so I couldn't see their faces.

The program was about to start by the time

Momma and Daddy sat down. Momma took Marcy from me. Marcy crawled off her lap and back onto mine.

"Spit," Marcy said.

I kissed her and tried to put her onto the seat next to mine. She crawled back onto my lap. I gave up. Marcy always does exactly what she wants to do. I noticed that Ms. Canales was watching us.

I barely listened to the program. I had to leave twice to take Marcy for a walk because she wouldn't sit still.

She couldn't seem to stop fidgeting during the program. She moved from Momma's lap to Daddy's lap to mine, and then started all over again. Ms. Canales looked over at us from time to time. The only time Marcy was quiet was when Taylor Parker sang "I Believe I Can Fly." I hated to admit it, but Taylor can really sing.

When it was time to meet with Ms. Canales, I was sweating like I had a fever. Ms. Canales asked my parents to come into the office instead of into our classroom. I found that very weird. She met with other parents in our classroom. The vice-principal, Mrs. Oliver, was waiting in the office.

My parents sat down and looked from Ms. Canales to Mrs. Oliver.

Mrs. Oliver said, "I'm only here to assist in facilitating this meeting."

Momma said, "Is something wrong?"

I sat up.

Ms. Canales said, "Well, I have had some problems with Sharie lately and I thought that this would be a good time to talk with you."

Daddy said, "Why didn't you call us? We could have dealt with any problem much earlier."

Ms. Canales said, "I understand your concern. But to be honest, at first I believed that there was a problem in your home."

Momma sat up. "What on earth would give you that idea?" she asked.

I listened as Ms. Canales explained that I had made it seem as though they made me babysit Marcy all night long. Then she told them about the forged note incident. During this time, Momma raised an eyebrow and looked at me. My Daddy's face looked like the sky before a thunderstorm.

"Don't you worry, Ms. Canales, we will speak with Sharie. I promise that she will not give you any more problems. She will turn in all her homework and become a model student. I can guarantee that. Right, Sharie?" Daddy said, staring at me.

"Yes, sir," I said softly.

"We can only apologize for our daughter's behavior," Momma said.

"Before you go, I want to say one thing in Sharie's defense," Ms. Canales said.

"I noticed during the program how attached your baby is to Sharie."

"Yes," Momma said with a smile. "Marcy is crazy about Sharie."

"Well," Ms. Canales said. "You might keep that in mind when you talk with Sharie about her behavior. It's difficult to concentrate in class when you're sleepy. Maybe some of Sharie's problems can be solved by figuring out how she can get more sleep at night."

"We understand," Daddy said. "We'll discuss this and let you know what we come up with."

"Great," Ms. Canales said. "Sharie's a wonderful and very talented student. I know that by working together we can help her succeed."

I couldn't believe that Ms. Canales thought I was a wonderful student! I started to feel a little better. Marcy tugged on my arm and pulled me toward the door. She was ready to go for another walk.

"I'll take her," I said.

"Thanks," Momma said.

I grabbed Marcy's hand and she pulled me along. I had to laugh.

On the way home, no one said anything.

But when we got home, Daddy said, "We are so disappointed in your behavior at school, Sharie."

"Disappointed isn't a good way to describe it," Momma said. "Why didn't you come and talk to us about the problems you've been having?"

I burst into tears. "I feel like you've forgotten about me. Everything is about the baby or Sandra. It was bad enough before the baby came, but now it's even worse. And I've lost my best friend and you haven't even noticed."

"Sharie," Momma said, hugging me, "you know we love you."

"You don't understand," I said. "Since the baby came you spend all your time with her. It's always about Marcy."

Daddy said, "Marcy's a baby, Sharie. You're almost twelve. Do you want us to carry you around on our hip?"

"No," I said, sniffling.

"Listen, it's late. We'll talk about this tomorrow. Let's go to bed."

Momma and Daddy both tucked me in. Marcy was already asleep. I hoped she'd stay that way. I was too tired to rock her tonight.

When they turned out the light and left the room, I started to cry again. I couldn't help it. I felt so mixed-up and confused.

I heard a tap on the door. I quickly pulled the sheet up over my head. I didn't want them to see me still crying. I waited for Momma to come through the door.

Instead, Sandra peeked in. "Can I come in?" she asked.

"Why? So you can tease me? I know you heard us, so you know they tucked me in. Go ahead and laugh."

"I'm not laughing, unless they gave you a bottle, too," she said, stepping into the room.

I smiled a little. "No, they didn't."

"Good," Sandra said. "I was beginning to worry for a minute when I heard Daddy coming back from the kitchen."

"He brought me some milk in a glass."

Sandra sat down on my bed. "Listen, I want to tell you something."

"Go ahead," I said. I was pretty sure she would say something to hurt my feelings even more. It didn't matter — I couldn't cry any more than I already had.

"When you were born, I tried to sell you," Sandra said.

"What?" I asked her. "What do you mean?"

"I was only two years old, but I knew I didn't like all the attention you were getting. So whenever some-one came to visit us, I would ask them if they were interested in buying a baby. I figured that if Momma and Daddy got some money for you, they wouldn't mind so much that you were gone."

I laughed. "You're serious?"

"Yes. Until you came along, I had all the attention. You were always crying or getting into something. And all they could talk about was how cute and adorable you were.

"Then, as we got older, you tore up all my paper dolls. You wrote on my books and climbed all over my bed. You know how much I hate people on my bed."

"You're on my bed now," I said, giggling.

"Yeah, but this is different."

"So what happened? Did anyone ever buy me?"

"That was the problem. No one would give me money for you. I thought I really hated you."

Then Sandra did something I never thought she'd do in a million years. She leaned over and kissed me on the forehead. If I hadn't been lying in bed I probably would have fainted.

"Did you just kiss me?" I asked.

"You dodo-head — I love you. I know I give you a

hard time, but that's what big sisters do. I don't hate you. I hate how messy you keep your room. But you, you're my little sister. I could never hate you. I just want you to know that one day, you'll look at Marcy and think, gosh I love that little girl, because that's what happened to me."

And just like that, she left the room. I lay there staring at the ceiling until I fell asleep. What a day! Ms. Canales thought I was talented and Sandra said she loves me.

Chapter Eight

〰〰〰〰〰〰〰〰〰〰〰〰〰〰〰〰

Surprise, Surprise, Surprise

Saturday morning is the only day Daddy allows us to sleep late. In his military world, that's until eight o'clock. Today, he woke me up at six o'clock. I thought he was getting me up early as punishment for my behavior at school. I was wrong.

"Rise and shine, baby girl," he said. "We've got a surprise project to do today."

I groaned and turned over. "Daddy, please let me sleep. I'm tired."

"I know, Sweet Pea, but your mother and I have decided the problem is that we don't spend enough individual time with each of you girls. So from now on, we're taking turns finding activities we can do together."

"What are we going to do today?" I asked sleepily.

"We're going to turn the attic into your new bedroom," Daddy said.

I sat up. I couldn't believe what I was hearing.

"I'm getting my own room?" I asked.

"That's right," Daddy said. "We're going to clean out the attic and store that stuff in the garage. Then we'll paint the room and move your bedroom furniture up there. Marcy will probably stop waking up at night if she knows that you're not there to rock her and sing to her. What do you think?"

"Can I have my computer and desk back?" I asked.

"Of course," Daddy said. "We'll move everything upstairs."

I smiled, climbed out of bed, and ran into the bathroom to get ready. Sandra and Marcy were still asleep. Momma was sitting at the kitchen table having a cup of coffee when I came downstairs.

"Momma," I said as I got a cereal bowl, "I can't believe I get to have my own room again."

"It's time that you got a good night's sleep," she said, smiling. "Marcy will get used to sleeping alone. We know it's been hard for you and we appreciate your help. Now we just want you to do well in school again."

"I will, Momma," I said.

"Your daddy's already moving things to the garage. I think you'll like having your room in the attic."

"I know I will," I said. "It will be like sleeping in a tree house."

"And the best part about it is that you can close the door to the stairway and Marcy can't get into your room."

I forgot about that part. The only stairway to the attic is in the kitchen, but Marcy can't open the door to get to it. Now she won't be able to come into my room. Having my room in the attic was a great idea!

As soon as I finished breakfast, I headed up the creaky stairs to the attic. Daddy had already boxed up most of the Christmas decorations we had stored up there. The attic isn't very big, but it was the perfect size for me. I looked out of the window. I could see for miles.

"What do you think?" Daddy said. "Will this work for you?"

"It's perfect," I said. "Thanks, Daddy."

"No problem," Daddy said. "We should have thought of this a long time ago. Just promise me one thing, Sharie."

"Yes, sir?"

"From now on, come and talk with us when you're having problems," Daddy said. "We don't want to hear about them from your teacher."

"Okay, Daddy," I said. "I'm sorry."

"Well, it's a new day and we're starting fresh," Daddy said. "Grab a box and let's get this room in shipshape."

"Yes, sir!"

I took a box and went downstairs. It took most of the morning to move everything out of the attic. Now I understand why Daddy wanted to get an early start.

After we moved everything to the garage, Daddy and I painted the attic walls a bright yellow. That's my favorite color. While we waited for the walls to dry, Momma and I went to Big Mart to buy new, yellow-flowered curtains and a matching bedspread for my room. I also got a new flowered trash can, a bookshelf, and some pictures. I usually hate to shop, but I had to admit that we had a good time.

Then Daddy and I moved my furniture upstairs. I couldn't help but smile when I moved my computer out of Sandra's room and into my new room. Now, she'd have to ask me for permission to use it instead of the other way around. I was smiling at the thought of Sandra begging me for permission until Daddy said they were planning on buying Sandra a laptop of her own. She needs one so that she can do her homework while she's waiting at her music lesson or traveling to and from school activities. Oh, well, at least I have my old computer again.

We moved all of Marcy's things out of Sandra's room and into my old room. Now everyone has their own room.

Momma and I hung up my new curtains. I made my bed and put the new bedspread on it. We hung my pictures on the walls. My new room looked beautiful!

The attic only has one tiny closet. Soon it was full. It's a good thing I don't have very many clothes! Sandra's stuff would never fit in there.

"It just needs one more thing and then it will be finished," Momma said.

"What?" I asked. I looked around. My desk and computer were near the window. My bed was against the wall and my dresser was next to the closet. It's a tiny room, but the yellow walls and new curtains and bedspread made it look bright and cheerful. I couldn't think of anything that was missing.

"I'll be right back," Momma said.

She went downstairs. I put my books on the bookshelf. Then I sat at my desk and looked out of the window. If I had known that Momma and Daddy would give me my own room, I would have told them a long time ago about being sleepy in class. Daddy was right — I should have talked to them first instead of waiting until Ms. Canales had to tell them. I'd never do that again.

I could hear the attic stairs creaking as Momma and Daddy came back up. Sandra and Marcy were right behind them. My room was crowded now. Marcy tried to get down, but Sandra wouldn't let her.

"Wow!" Sandra said. "This is cute!"

"I love it," I said.

"It's really nice," Daddy said. "It's amazing what a coat of paint can do."

"Okay," Momma said. "One last thing and Sharie's new room will be finished."

Momma was holding a picture in her hand. It was a family portrait. She put the picture on my desk. It was the new one we had taken at the Photomat.

"Perfect," Daddy said, smiling. "Just a little reminder of the people who love you most."

I hugged Momma and Daddy. Marcy leaned over and gave me a slobbery kiss. Yuck! I wiped my face, but I couldn't help smiling. Sandra laughed.

"Thanks for everything," I said. "I love my new room."

"You're welcome," Daddy said. "Let's keep it clean up here, okay?"

"I'll try," I said.

"That'll be the day," Sandra said, smiling.

After everyone went back downstairs, I looked out of the window for a long time. This day had been full of surprises. I looked around my new room. It was the first room I'd ever had that I had decorated with brand-new things. Usually, I just used leftover things that Momma had lying around. I thought it looked beautiful. I fell asleep with a smile on my face.

On Monday morning, Ms. Canales asked me to wait after class was over. Hannah looked worried as she passed by. It made me feel good that she cared I might be in trouble.

"How did things go this weekend?" Ms. Canales asked.

"My parents moved my room to the attic," I said. "Now everyone has their own room. Momma said Marcy woke up during the night on Saturday, but when she saw I wasn't there, she went right back to sleep. She didn't wake up at all last night."

"That's good news," Ms. Canales said. "I asked your parents to find a way to give you your own space. I'm glad they were able to come up with a solution to your problem. I noticed you were alert in class and that you finished your homework, too."

"I'm trying to do better," I said.

"Well, keep up the good work," Ms. Canales said. "See you tomorrow."

" 'Bye, and thanks for everything," I said.

"You're welcome," Ms. Canales said.

Hannah and Taylor were standing by my locker. I walked around them and put my books inside. I was hoping Hannah would be waiting for me alone. I should have known that her new best friend would be with her.

"Hey, do you want to hang out with us today?" Hannah asked.

"I don't think so," I said. "Three's a crowd."

"Don't be silly," Taylor said. "I want to be your

94

friend. Hannah tells me that you write plays. I'd like to read some of them. Would you mind?"

"I guess not," I said.

"Great, can we come over your house?" asked Hannah.

"I didn't ask my mom if I could have company to-day," I said.

"You can call her," Hannah said. "Come on, Sharie. I miss talking to you."

I stopped putting things in my locker and looked at Hannah. She seemed sad. I realized that I missed her, too. I decided to stop acting this way. It wasn't the real me, anyway. I'd never been jealous of anyone before.

"Come on, let's call your mom," said Taylor. "That is, if you don't mind me coming over."

I wondered why was she being so nice to me. I certainly hadn't been very nice to her.

"There's really not much to do at my house," I said.

"We could go over the play you gave Hannah," Taylor said.

"I don't know," I said. "The last play I wrote wasn't very good."

They both giggled. "What's so funny?" I asked.

"We're laughing because when I read it I told Hannah that I'd love to play the lead part of the unpopular girl. It would be fun," Taylor said.

"And I could play the role of the popular girl," Hannah said.

"You're kidding me, right?" I said.

"No," Hannah said. "Taylor and I acted it out. It was fun!"

"Wow, I didn't know that," I said.

"I always get the same parts over and over," Taylor said. "It would be fun to play someone like the girl in your play."

"So can we come over? My mom is picking us up today. She can drop us off at your house," Hannah said.

I couldn't help but smile. I felt better than I had in months. That ugly jealous feeling I had been carrying around since Taylor arrived at our school disappeared.

"Let's call my mom and ask," I said, still wondering if this could work out.

I called home. Hannah talked to Momma since she had a better chance of getting a yes. Momma was happy that Hannah and I were friends again. She said yes right away.

When we got to my house, Momma made us a snack. We could barely talk because Marcy was crawling around our legs under the table.

"Sometimes my sisters drive me crazy," I said.

"My baby sisters are worse," Taylor said. "Aren't they, Hannah?"

"I don't know," Hannah said. "I like them."

"Yuck," Taylor and I said at the same time. We both laughed.

"Jinxes, jinxes, you owe me a drink," Taylor and I said at the same time. We laughed again and toasted each other with our milk glasses.

Hannah picked up Marcy and played patty-cake with her. Hannah's an only child. I think that's why she loves coming over to my house so much. It would be different if she had a little sister climbing all over her every day. Momma finally took Marcy into her room to play. We finished our snack, and I took Hannah and Taylor up to my room.

"This is so cool!" Hannah said as she looked around my room.

"It's like you have your own private tree house," Taylor said as she looked out the window.

"The best part is that Marcy can't get up here," I said.

I sat on the bed and watched Taylor and Hannah act out my play. Then we talked about the changes we needed to make. I worked on revising the play while Taylor and Hannah read my other stories.

As I worked on the play, I realized that the lead character's good qualities must outshine any flaws she might have. The person watching the play should like the lead character. Once I'd heard the play read aloud, I realized that the person I created wasn't the real Hannah Lowenstein, after all. It was all the negative, untrue things that people thought about her.

Now, I created the real Hannah: witty, smart, and willing to stick her neck out for a new friend. When I was finished, I gave the revised play to Taylor and Hannah to read.

I held my breath as they read it. I wanted to hear what Hannah had to say, and yet I didn't want to hear it. I was afraid she wouldn't like my revision.

"This is very good. I can't believe someone as popular as you could understand how the lead character feels," said Taylor.

"Popular? Me?" I asked.

"Sure! Hannah told me that you were very popular and you still wanted to be her friend even though she wasn't that popular."

"Hannah told you that?" I asked. And all this time I thought Hannah had completely abandoned me.

"Yes. Hannah told me all about your other play, too. I thought the way you divided the lead role between her and Caitlin was brilliant. Hannah talks about you all the time."

I smiled at Hannah. I never realized that she had missed me just as much as I had missed her.

"Hannah did a great job in the play," I said. "She's a wonderful actress."

"I know," Taylor said. "She's as good as anyone I've worked with in California."

Hannah's face was almost as red as her hair.

Taylor and I laughed. Hannah laughed, too. I was happier than I had been in weeks. It was good to laugh with my friends in my new room. I was starting to feel like my old self again.

Chapter Nine

The Trouble with Tests

"Our first standardized test is this Friday," Ms. Canales said. "We're going to take some practice tests this week so you can prepare."

Everyone groaned. I had been looking out the window, thinking about my play. What had Ms. Canales just said? I got scared when she began passing out No. 2 pencils. Oh, no, practice tests! My mind went blank. My mouth felt dry. I felt like I was going to be sick. I hate taking these tests!

"Now, class, it's important to follow the rules," Ms. Canales said. "Do exactly as I say. Clear your desks of everything except a pencil and a booklet. Do not open the booklet until I tell you to do so. Understood? Is everyone ready?"

I opened my book to see if the questions were hard.

"Why are you opening the booklet, Sharie?" Ms. Canales asked. "Didn't you hear my instructions?"

"No, ma'am," I said. The class started to giggle. Why didn't I listen?

Ms. Canales said, "Let's start over." She repeated her instructions. "I want you to listen carefully. If I see anyone looking at the test before I say so, you're not going to be allowed to take it. Is that clear?"

I felt terrible. I was so busy thinking about my play that I'd been caught not paying attention again. I'd promised Ms. Canales after the parent-teacher conference that I'd try harder in class. I'd been doing pretty well, until today.

Ms. Canales walked around the class as she explained the practice test.

"You have fifteen minutes for the first section. When I say 'stop,' put down your pencils immediately and leave them down. Everyone understand? Okay, open your booklet and begin."

I worked on the test until Ms. Canales said to stop. I put my pencil down, but it rolled off my desk and onto the floor. When I tried to catch it, I knocked over my dictionary and my geography book that were on top of my backpack onto the floor. The books fell over with a loud crash. Some of the kids laughed as I struggled to pick them up.

Ms. Canales just shook her head. "Sharie Johnson! What's the problem?"

"I don't know," I said softly.

But I knew what was wrong. I'm afraid of taking the test. I've been afraid of standardized tests since I took the first one years ago.

During dinner that night, I told Momma and Daddy that I didn't feel well enough to go to school the next day. I didn't want to take any more practice tests.

"Oh, no, Sharie. Isn't Friday the day you have all your tests?" Momma asked. "There was a note about it in the PTA bulletin."

"Yes," I said. "We had a practice test today."

"How did you do?" Daddy asked.

"Okay, I guess," I said. "I was really nervous."

"You always get a little nervous," Daddy said. "Just try to relax. You're not sick. You'll do fine on the real test."

"I hope so," I said.

When it was time to go to bed, I couldn't stop worrying about Friday's test. I don't know why I'm not able to just listen and follow directions. My brain seems to cut off as soon as I pick up my No. 2 pencil.

I heard someone coming up the creaky stairs to my room. Those stairs are better than a doorbell. I always know when someone is coming. There was a knock on my door.

"Yes," I said. "Come in, Momma." I figured she wanted to say good night. Ever since I moved to the attic, either Momma or Daddy came to talk with me before I went to bed.

Sandra stuck her head in the door. "It's me," she said.

"What's up?" I said.

"I wanted to give you something."

I sat up. Sandra wanting to give me something is usually not a good sign.

"Does it bite?" I asked her.

"No, silly," she said, stepping into my room. "Here." She handed me a booklet.

I read the cover, "Simple Tips for Taking Standardized Tests."

"I used to hate taking those tests," Sandra said. "Sometimes I was so scared that I couldn't hear the instructions. I mean, I could hear what the teacher was saying. But I couldn't concentrate."

"I know," I said. "I feel the same way. Ms. Canales was explaining the instructions today. I was so scared that I couldn't focus."

"I got this booklet at the library when I was in the fifth grade," Sandra said.

"And you kept it?" I asked.

"No, silly," Sandra said. "It was free to anyone who wanted a copy."

"Oh," I said. "That's good."

"Read it and try to follow the tips. If you don't understand something, ask me in the morning, okay?"

"Okay," I said. "Thanks, but how did you know I needed help taking my test?"

"You didn't eat your dessert," Sandra said. "I knew something was wrong if you skipped chocolate cake."

I threw my pillow at her. Sandra ducked, laughed, and went downstairs.

I opened the booklet and started to read. There was plenty of information that I hadn't thought about. Thanks to my big sister, I was going to ace this test.

The next day in class, I listened very carefully to the instructions. I opened the practice test and I put down my pencil when Ms. Canales said so.

After class, Hannah and Taylor were waiting for me by my locker.

"Look what Sandra gave me," I said to Hannah. "It's a booklet full of test-taking tips. Would you like to see it?"

"I can pass those tests without breaking a sweat," Hannah said. "You know that."

I felt a little hurt. I know how smart Hannah is,

but she didn't have to make me feel bad about my fear of tests.

"Well, I'm not that good with tests," Taylor said. "Let me see it."

I smiled at Taylor. Here she was, a television star who everyone wanted to be friends with. But she didn't do well on standardized tests, either.

"Maybe we can study the test-taking tips at my house," Taylor said. "Would you like to come over?"

"Sure," I said. "But I have to call my mother first."

"Well, my mom just got back into town, so I'm going home," Hannah said.

"Okay," I said. "See you tomorrow."

"See you, Hannah," Taylor said.

Taylor's mom was waiting for us when we came out of the building. Taylor and I climbed inside the car. I plopped down onto the plush leather seats. It was one of the nicest cars I had ever ridden in.

"Hi, Mom, this is Sharie Johnson," Taylor said. "She's going to call her mom to ask if she can come over today."

"Hello, Sharie," Mrs. Parker said. "Nice to meet you. Go ahead and give your mom a call."

Taylor got her bright blue cell phone out of the glove compartment. "Here's the phone, Sharie," she said.

I called Momma. When she found out we were studying for Friday's test, she said it was okay for me to visit until dinnertime.

"How'd school go today?" Mrs. Parker asked.

"Fine," we both said at the same time.

"Jinxes, jinxes, you owe me a drink!" I shouted.

Taylor giggled and got two juice boxes out of the built-in cooler in the backseat. We drank our juice and ate a box of raisins on the way to her house.

I couldn't believe how big Taylor's house is. It was even bigger than Caitlin's house, and hers is huge.

"You have a beautiful house, Mrs. Parker," I said.

"Thank you!" Mrs. Parker said. "Taylor tells me she wishes she had a room like yours. She says it's like a tree house!"

"Can I move my room up to the attic, Mom?" Taylor asked.

"I don't think our attic is as cool as Sharie's," Mrs. Parker laughed. "You can't stand up in there and you'd have to share it with a bunch of spiders."

Taylor and I laughed at the thought of her having spiders for roommates.

"You'd come to school covered with spiderwebs," I laughed.

"No one would want to sit near me because my spider roommates would crawl out of my backpack," Taylor giggled.

"I'd still sit with you," I said. "But I wouldn't sit very close. You could sit at one end of the table and I'd sit at the other."

"If I wanted to send you a note, I'd have to send it by spider mail," Taylor said.

"You two are really silly today," Mrs. Parker said. "Make sure you study as much as you giggle."

The inside of Taylor's house was as beautiful as the outside. When we walked into the kitchen, four tiny hands grabbed me around my knees. Two little girls, who had to be twins, almost knocked me down.

"Whee!" the girls sang. "Hey, what's your name? You came to play with us, right?"

The little girls joined hands and danced around me. Then they grabbed me by the hands and pulled me around the kitchen, laughing and giggling loudly.

Another little boy, who was younger than the twins, grabbed Taylor around the knees.

Except for the twins, Taylor and her brother and sisters didn't look the same. Their skin colors and their hair were all different.

"Leave me alone, Timmy," Taylor said. "And get off my friend, Cathy and Patty. I mean it."

"It's okay," I said, as Taylor pried the twins' sticky hands off my legs. "I'm used to it. My little sister acts the same way."

"Mother," Taylor called as she swung Timmy up to her hip, "could you come and get them, please?"

I had jelly handprints all over my jeans. Taylor handed me a napkin.

"I'm sorry," Taylor said. "That's why I like visiting friends after school. By the time I come home, they're almost ready for bed."

Taylor's mother took the twins and the brother into another room. Taylor and I went upstairs. When we finally got up to her room, I was exhausted.

"My sisters and brother can wear anybody out," Taylor said.

I sat down on a chaise lounge. The fabric had costumed dolls from around the world printed on it. I stared at the shelves in front of me, which were filled with dolls.

"Wow," I said. "You have the most dolls I've ever seen. They're beautiful. Do you ever play with them?"

"I used to. But now I play with my real dolls."

"Your real dolls? What do you mean?"

"Well," Taylor explained, "I was the only child until I was eight years old, when my parents adopted the twins. My father was adopted, and he's always said how important adoption is. Then they decided to adopt Timmy, too. There's never a moment's peace, but I love it. I like being a big sister. And we have a part-time maid who helps with the babysitting and the housework. It's not so bad."

"I know what you mean," I said. "Now that I have my own room, I don't mind my sisters so much, either."

"Yeah, having a place where you can hide is a good thing," Taylor laughed. "Come on, we better read the test booklet and take the practice tests. You have to go home soon."

"Okay," I said as I took the booklet out of my backpack.

Taylor and I read the simple tips in the front of the book. Many of them were things we already knew, like listening carefully and checking your answers. But there were other hints, too, like if questions are based on a reading passage, it's best to read the questions first, and then the passage.

"Okay," Taylor said. "I'll pretend I'm Ms. Canales and you can take the practice test. Then you can be Ms. Canales and give me the test."

"Okay," I said smiling.

Taylor acted exactly like Ms. Canales. I tried not to giggle and made myself focus on the instructions and the questions. When I finished, I went back over everything like the booklet suggested. Then, Taylor checked my answers.

"Good job," Taylor said. "Okay, now you pretend to be Ms. Canales."

I read the instructions in my best Ms. Canales voice. Taylor smiled at me, but followed the instructions carefully. Then she took the practice test and I checked it.

"Great, Taylor!" I said. "I think we're going to do really well on Friday."

"I think so, too," Taylor said. "I'm glad your sister gave you that booklet."

"Yeah, sometimes she's really nice to me," I said.

"I like having a brother and sisters," Taylor said.

"I guess I do, too," I said. "I've never been an only child, but I don't think I'd like it very much."

"You wouldn't," Taylor said. "Come on, we should ask my mom if she can take you home. It's getting late."

"Thanks for inviting me over, Taylor," I said.

"No, thank you!" Taylor said. "This is the first time I've ever taken a test without feeling nervous."

"Me, too!" I said.

Taylor and I smiled at each other. We have a lot in common. We both like acting and plays, we both have pesky sisters, and we both have to work hard to make good grades. It was nice to know that I wasn't the only one who had to work for my grades. Everything came so easily to Sandra and Hannah.

When I finally got home, I was tired.

"Spit, spit, spit," Marcy said as she pulled on my jeans.

I picked her up. "Kissy, kissy, kissy," I corrected. "Marcy, say kissy, kissy, kissy."

"Kissy!" Marcy said happily.

I gave her two big kisses on her cheek. She squealed, and I swung her around. I had to admit it, she is a sweet baby.

"I'm going to be a better big sister from now on. You'll see," I whispered to her.

At dinner, I didn't strap Marcy into her high chair. I held her on my lap.

"Want me to take the baby?" Momma asked.

"No, I've got her," I said, smiling.

"That's very nice of you, Sharie," said Daddy.

Sandra said, "She must want something."

"No, I don't," I said.

"Sandra, your sister is just trying to help out," said Daddy.

I couldn't believe it. Daddy was taking my side. My new, positive attitude was already working. Now I only had one more hurdle to cross. I wanted Hannah to be my best friend again. I just didn't know how to tell her.

The next day, Ms. Canales asked me to wait after class. I thought, *Oh, no, what now?*

"Sharie," Ms. Canales said, "I just want you to know I'm proud of you. You haven't been talking in class or passing notes to Hannah. And you followed the instructions on the last practice test perfectly."

"Thanks," I said, as tears welled in my eyes.

"What's the matter?" Ms. Canales said. "I gave you a compliment."

"It's just that I haven't been talking or passing notes to Hannah because she's not my best friend anymore. Not that I would talk or pass notes or anything. I'm not going to do that anymore."

"Listen, Sharie," Ms. Canales said, "every friendship gets tested. Don't worry. I'm sure Hannah will come around."

"But what if she doesn't?" I asked.

"She will. Hannah has always been loyal to you."

Ms. Canales's observation made me feel worse. Hannah always *had* been loyal to me. When I first came to Austin, Hannah was the only person who wanted to be my friend. All the other kids ignored me. I didn't realize what a good friend I had until she decided to be friends with someone else. I'd never told Hannah how much she meant to me. That's it! I'd write Hannah a letter and tell her that I wanted to be best friends again.

Chapter Ten

The Meaning of Friendship

For the next two days, I worked on my letter to Hannah. I started by thanking her for being nice to me when no one else wanted to be my friend. I thanked her for defending me when others said mean things about me. I thanked Hannah for every kind thing she had ever done for me.

I read what I had written and thought about all the fun Hannah and I used to have. It made me sad that Hannah no longer wanted to come over for the weekend. The more I thought about Hannah, the more I realized how she was the one who had been a good friend, not me.

I finished the letter and asked Hannah to forgive

me for acting so mean. I signed the letter B.F.F.E., best friends forever. All I could do was hope for the best. I put the letter into my backpack and climbed into bed. Then I heard the stairs squeaking.

"Ahoy, matey!" Daddy said as he flicked the light switch off and on. "It's time for lights out!"

"Wait, Daddy," I said. "I need to ask you something."

Daddy switched the light on and sat down on the end of the bed.

"What's the matter?"

"Well," I said. "Hannah and I are friends again, but we're not best friends like we used to be."

"She doesn't come over as much as she did before," Daddy said. "Your momma and I miss having her around."

"I miss her, too," I said. I never thought that Daddy and Momma missed Hannah. I forgot how much time she spent over here.

"I wrote her a letter and told her that I was sorry for being so jealous of her and Taylor," I said.

"That's a good thing to do," Daddy said. "Did you

tell her that you want to be best friends again?" Daddy asked.

"Yes," I said.

"You were jealous of Hannah and Taylor's friendship, but you've always had Annette as a best friend, too," Daddy pointed out. "Hannah never seemed to mind that Annette was also your best friend."

I'd never thought about that. Annette was my best friend when we lived in Kansas and I still thought of her as my best friend now. Even though Hannah knows about Annette, she never acted jealous. But the minute Hannah made friends with Taylor, I got mad. I didn't look at it that way until now.

"You're right," I said. "It's my fault that Hannah and I aren't good friends anymore."

"Well, maybe after she reads your letter, things will get back to normal," Daddy said.

"No, I want things to be different," I said.

"Why?" Daddy asked.

"Because I don't want to act jealous like that again," I said. "I like Taylor and I want all of us to be friends."

"That's my girl," Daddy said. "Now g[...]
Your big test is tomorrow and you need your [...]
Everything will work out just fine, you'll see."

Daddy gave me a big hug and turned off the light.
I fell asleep before he reached the bottom of the
stairs.

The next day, I had butterflies in my stomach. I gave
Hannah my letter as soon as she walked into the
room. I saw her read it, but I didn't have time to talk
to her because it was test day. As soon as we finished
the morning assembly, we put everything away and
got ready to take our tests.

Taylor smiled at me when Ms. Canales started
reading the instructions. I could tell she was feeling a
little nervous, too. I had reread the test-tip booklet
on the bus this morning. During the test, I tried to remember everything the booklet said to do.

When Ms. Canales told us to stop and put down
our pencils, I felt relieved. The test was finally over
and I knew I'd done a good job answering the questions.

I turned around to look at Taylor. She was smiling, too.

"Class, the rest of the day will be a free period," Ms. Canales said. "You may talk in low voices, quietly play games, or go to the library and read. Good job on your tests. Thank you for following my instructions."

Ms. Canales looked at me and smiled when she said the last part. I smiled back.

Everyone started to move around the classroom. I pulled my chair over to Hannah's desk. She was writing something and didn't look at me when I sat down. Taylor leaned over to talk to me.

"How do you think you did on the test?" Taylor asked.

"Great!" I said. "What about you?"

"I think I did pretty well, too," Taylor said. "I'm just glad it's over. Those test tips really helped."

"They sure did," I said.

"I'm going to the library," Taylor said. "Do you two want to go with me?"

Hannah and I looked at each other. She shook her head.

"Maybe we'll come down later," I said.

Taylor looked at us and smiled.

"Okay," Taylor said. "I'll see you later."

Taylor got in line with a few others who were going to the library.

"Hannah," I said. "Did you read my letter?"

"Yes," Hannah said. She still wouldn't look at me. I thought that maybe she had decided that she didn't want to be best friends anymore.

Suddenly, Hannah pushed a folded sheet of paper toward me. Inside there was a multicolored, braided friendship bracelet. The note read:

B.F.F.E. BEST FRIENDS FOREVER! HANNAH AND SHARIE!

I smiled at Hannah. We had started making the bracelets the last time she spent the night at my house. I never finished hers, but she finished mine.

Hannah helped me tie the bracelet around my wrist.

"I'll finish your bracelet this weekend — I promise," I said.

"Can I come over to help you?" Hannah asked.

"Sure!" I said. "And while we're at it, we can make one for Taylor."

"And one for Annette, too," Hannah said with a smile.

"Let's go to the library," I said. "Our new best friend is waiting for us."